Another Sommer-Time Story™

The RICHEST POOR KID

by Carl Sommer
Illustrated by Jorge Martinez

Advance PUBLISHING, INC. • HOUSTON

Permissions
Advance Publishing, Inc.
6950 Fulton St.
Houston, TX 77022

www.advancepublishing.com

First Edition
Printed in Malaysia

Library of Congress Cataloging-in-Publication Data

Sommer, Carl.
  The richest poor kid / by Carl Sommer ; illustrated by Jorge Martinez.
      p. cm. -- (Another Sommer-time story)
  Summary: Randy hates being poor, so when he is magically granted two wishes, the first thing he wishes is for everything he touches to turn to gold.
  ISBN-13: 978-1-57537-025-5 (hardcover : alk. paper)
  ISBN-10: 1-57537-025-5 (hardcover : alk. paper)
  ISBN-13: 978-1-57537-074-3 (library binding : alk. paper)
  ISBN-10: 1-57537-074-3 (library binding : alk. paper) [1. Family life--Fiction. 2. Wishes--Fiction. 3. Gold--Fiction.] I. Martinez, Jorge,
1951- ill. II. Title.

  PZ7.S696235Ri 2007
  [E]--dc22

                                                                        2006028448

The RICHEST POOR KID

Randy had an old problem. Everything he had was *old*—and to Randy it was a big, BIG problem.

Randy lived in an old wooden house. It was clean, but it was much too old for Randy. His friends lived in beautiful brick houses.

Randy had an old bicycle and a few old toys, but his neighbor Mike had a new bike and lots of new toys. Whenever Mike saw Randy riding his old bike, he yelled, "Get your piece of junk off the

road!" Then he laughed at Randy for riding his old bike.

This made Randy furious. When Randy got out of sight, he would give his old bike a swift hard kick, and yell, "Ohhhhh!!!! How I wish I were rich! I'd buy a new bike and get rid of this old piece of junk!"

"Why can't I get new clothes?" Randy always complained. "And why do I always have to wear hand-me-downs from my brother?"

When Randy rode in their old family car, he always grumbled, "Everything I have is old, old, OLD!!! How I *wish* I were rich! Then I'd get *everything* NEW!"

One day Randy asked his sister, "Why are we so poor?"

"Dad died when you were three years old," explained his sister, "now Mom has to work to support us. Mom barely makes enough money to pay for rent and food, so there's never any money left for new things."

Then Mom walked in and gave Randy a big hug. Mom always gave her children lots and lots of love.

In the evenings, Mom had her children read books from the library. When they were finished reading, they sat together and talked. Mom often remarked, "I want you to make a better life for yourself, but as long as we have food and clothing, we should be happy and content."

"Not me!" Randy always mumbled to himself. "Look at my friends. They have new things, and they're always happy. I have old things, and I'm always miserable!"

There was another thing that made Randy mad—really mad. His mom believed that teaching children how to work would help them when they became older. She often said, "Learning to work is the path to success."

Randy and his brother and sister had to do all

kinds of chores. They cleaned the dishes, vacuumed the floors, dusted the furniture, took out the garbage, helped with the laundry, weeded the garden, mowed the lawn, and did whatever else was needed.

Randy often complained, "Look at Mike. He never works, but *I* have to do all kinds of work!"

One day Mike saw Randy weeding the garden. "Look at the poor servant boy," he yelled. Then he let out a loud laugh and said, "Make sure you're pulling out all the weeds."

Randy, his face red with anger, groaned, "Ohhhh!!!! If only I were rich! Then I'd get someone to do *all* my work. Then no one would *ever* laugh at me again!"

Randy hated to be corrected. Whenever his teacher said, "To become successful you must learn how to work," Randy got angry.

When his teacher repeated what his mom had tried to teach him, "Remember, things don't bring happiness. If you have a loving home, clothes to wear, and food to eat, you should be happy." Randy became furious. "No way!" he grumbled.

"Happiness comes by having *new* things!"

Then Randy would close his eyes and dream, "I wish my pockets were filled with gold so I could buy anything I want. Then I'd throw away all my old junk and buy everything new. Then no one could ever tease me again. Ohhhh!!!! How I *wish* I were rich! Then I'd be the *happiest* kid in the *whole* world!"

After doing his chores one night, Randy threw himself on his bed and groaned, "Ohhhhh!!!!! If only I were rich, I'd be so happy. I'd never have a sad day in my life again!"

Randy had not done anything unusual that day—nothing that would explain what was about to happen.

Suddenly, the floor shook, a flash of lightning lit up the room, and a deafening blast of thunder shook the house. It seemed as if the sun itself had burst into his room.

Randy sat up straight in his bed. His eyes nearly bolted out of their sockets. By his window was a cloud with a man's face!

The voice spoke slowly, "Randy, you can wish for anything you want."

Then the voice warned, "But don't forget! You get only *two* wishes, so be *extremely* careful for what you wish."

Randy did not waste a second. He knew exactly what he wanted. He blurted out, "I wish *everything* I touch turns to gold!"

Suddenly, there was a loud noise. Randy

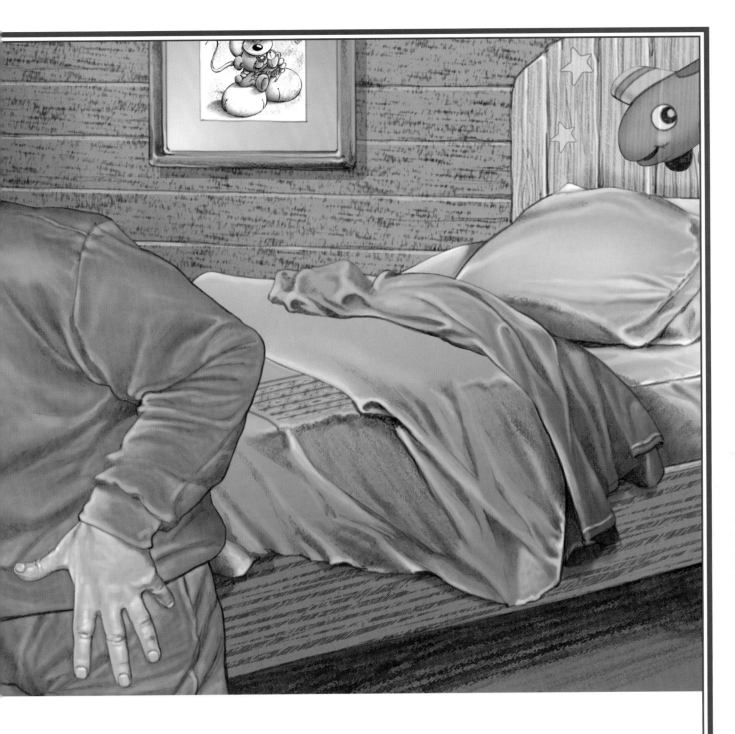

blinked, and when he opened his eyes, he was all alone. He rubbed his eyes and asked, "Did something really happen, or was it just a dream?"

Without another thought, Randy jumped out of bed and dashed across the room to touch the first thing he saw. "I sure hope my wish comes true!"

When Randy's hand touched a lamp, in a flash the lamp turned to gold!

Randy could not believe his eyes. He pinched himself. He was awake!

Randy held up his gold lamp and shouted at the top of his voice, "I'm rich! I'm really rich! Now I can buy everything new! This is the *happiest* day of my life!"

Randy saw his old soccer ball. He picked it up and it instantly turned into gold. He was shocked. Then he yelled, "I've got a gold soccer ball!"

Randy had never been so happy. He jumped up and down and danced around the room, shouting, "Hurrayyyy!!!! I'm rich!!! I'm rich!!! Hurrayyyy!!!!"

Randy raced into the living room and touched the chair. It turned to gold! "Everything I touch turns to gold!" he shouted. "I'm the *happiest* kid in the *whole* world!"

Randy ran around the room touching everything he could find. And everything he touched turned to pure gold!

"I can't wait until I get to a store," he exclaimed. "I'm throwing all my old things away. I'm buying *everything* new!

"I'll get a gold bike that will make Mike's bike look like a piece of junk. When I see him on his bike, I'll yell, 'Get your cheap piece of junk off the road!'"

"Look!" yelled Randy while still thinking about his gold bike, "My model plane." He rushed over and touched it. "This is great!" he shouted as he watched his plane turn to gold.

Running around the room and turning every-thing to gold made Randy hungry. "I'm going to the kitchen to get something to eat," he said.

Randy skipped into the kitchen and spotted some apples. "Good," he said. "I'll eat an apple."

Randy bit down hard on the apple. "Ouchhh!!!"
he screamed.
The apple had turned to gold!

"Oh, I forgot," said Randy. "Everything I touch turns to gold. But that's not a problem."

Randy bent over the bowl and began eating another apple. He put his hands behind his back to make sure he did not touch the apple with his hands. "This isn't easy," he said, "but I don't mind. I'm extremely rich, and that's the *most* important thing in life!"

Randy became thirsty. He picked up a cup and it immediately turned to gold. "That's okay," he said smiling. "I'll just fill the gold cup with some grape juice."

When he opened the refrigerator, the refrigerator turned to gold. "Am I ever lucky!" Randy shouted. "Everything I touch turns to gold!"

"This grape juice is coming out slowly," said Randy. "I'll open the spout."

As he opened the spout, he accidentally touched the juice—the juice turned to gold. Now Randy began to worry. "How am I going to get a drink? I'm thirsty!"

He sat there thinking. Suddenly he got an idea. "It's simple," he said.

He put his head on the faucet and pushed it. As he sipped the water he reminded himself, "I've got to be very careful not to touch the water."

While drinking the water Randy began feeling more and more miserable. "All this gold isn't making me happy anymore," he grumbled.

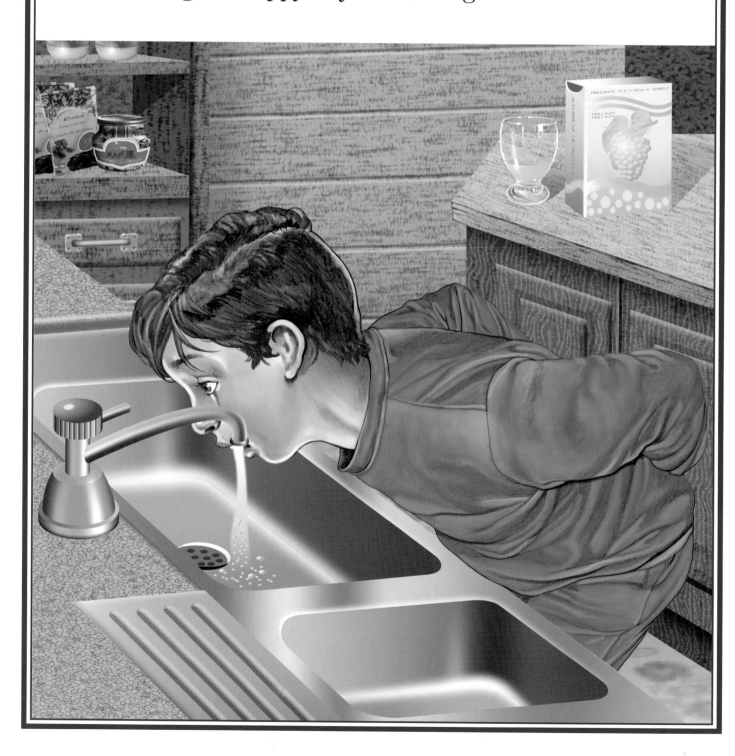

Then he looked at all the gold around him.
"Why am I getting so sad?" he asked. "I'm rich!"

Randy gathered some of the gold objects and
placed them on his desk. "Look at all *my* gold!"
he exclaimed. "Now *I* can buy anything *I* want!"

When Randy heard Sandy, his beloved dog,
he bent down and called, "Come, Sandy! Come!"

Sandy raced across the room.

When Sandy jumped on his lap, Randy patted Sandy and said, "Good girl."

Then he screamed at the top of his voice, "OH NOOOOO!!!!!"

Sandy began turning to gold!

Randy plopped into his gold chair and cried, "Ohhhhh!!!!! How I wish I could have my Sandy back! Why does everything I touch turn to gold? This is the worst day of my life! I'm the richest kid in the whole world, but I'm also the most miserable kid in the whole world!"

Randy looked at his gold dog and all the gold objects in his room. Then he walked into the kitchen and saw the gold apple, the gold cup, the gold juice, and the gold refrigerator. He shook his head and said, "Look at me! I'm the richest poor kid."

Then he remembered what his mom and teacher had tried to tell him. "Things don't bring happiness. If you have a loving home, clothes to wear, and food to eat, you have all you need to be happy."

"They're absolutely right," said Randy shaking his head. "Look at me. I can turn everything to gold, but I'm the most miserable kid in the *whole* world. All I want is to have my dog back and to be able to drink a glass of water!"

Suddenly, Randy jumped up and exclaimed, "I get one more wish! I could wish to have my dog back!"

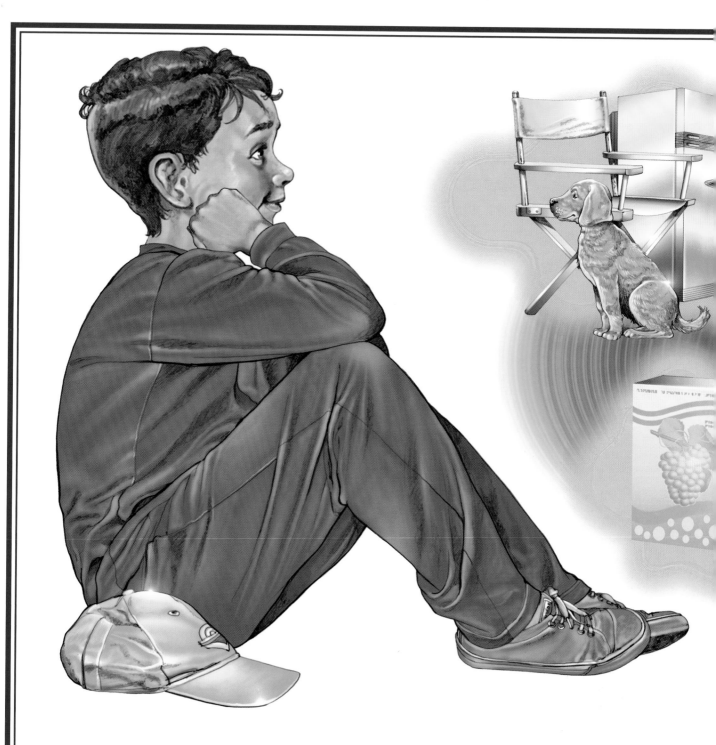

All of a sudden fear gripped Randy and sweat began pouring down his face. "What if nothing happens and everything stays this way forever? Did I really get two wishes?"

Randy plopped on the floor and began to think how terrible it would be if everything in his house turned to gold. "I could never hug my mom again," he groaned, "or hold an ice cream cone, or play

soccer, or play with Sandy. Oh, how I *hate* that everything I touch turns to gold. What a terrible, miserable life!"

Then Randy remembered the voice had warned him, "Be *extremely* careful for what you wish."

Suddenly, his eyes lit up. "I may *have* another chance!" Then he said, "If I have another chance, I've got to be very, very careful for what I wish."

Then Randy became excited, "I can wish for
everything to be the way it was before! Then I can
once again run and play ball and do other fun
things."

Tears began streaming down his face. "I don't
care if I *ever* get anything new again for the rest

of my life. I just want to live the way I used to."

Knowing it would be his last chance to make a wish, Randy sat there and thought. After thinking a long time on what he should say, he said very slowly and carefully, "I…wish…everything…would…be…like…it…was…before!"

Suddenly, there was a flash of lightning, then a loud blast of thunder that shook the house. Smoke filled the room.

When the smoke settled, everything Randy had touched became normal again. The chair turned into wood, his soccer ball became soft, and once

again Randy could play with all his games.

Best of all, Sandy jumped on his lap and began licking his face. Randy was so happy that he hugged Sandy and danced around the room, shouting over and over again, "This is the happiest day of my life!"

While Randy was shouting and jumping up and down for joy, he suddenly woke up. The noise caused Mom and Sandy to rush into his room. Sandy jumped on his bed and began licking his face.

"Are you okay?" asked Mom.

"You didn't turn to gold?" asked Randy.

"Of course not," laughed Mom.

"I dreamt that everything I touched turned to gold," explained Randy, as he held Sandy close in

his arms. "I thought that would make me happy, but I was miserable. Now I'm thankful for the way I live and even for my old toys. I'm also thankful for having a real dog and the best mom in the whole world."

Then he reached out and gave his mom a giant hug. "I love you, Mom! Now I know that even though we don't have money, I'm the richest poor kid because I have a mom like you."

"Thank you," said Mom as she kissed Randy and wiped tears from her eyes.

The next day when Mike laughed at Randy for working so hard, he said to Mike, "You can laugh all you want. It doesn't bother me."